To Cyril,
Congratulations on
a wonderful year in
Kindergarten
♡ Mrs. Conroy

King of the Skies

story by

Rukhsana Khan

art by

Laura Fernandez & Rick Jacobson

North Winds Press

A Division of Scholastic Canada Ltd.

The paintings for this book were created in oil on canvas.

This book was designed in QuarkXPress, with type set in 16 point Hiroshige Book.

National Library of Canada Cataloguing in Publication Data

Khan, Rukhsana
King of the skies

ISBN 0-439-98725-3

I. Jacobson, Rick. II. Fernandez, Laura. III. Title.

PS8571.H42K56 2001   jC813'.54   C2001-930536-2
PZ7.K42Ki 2001

5 4 3 2 1   Printed and bound in Canada   1 2 3 4 /0

For my father, Muhammad Anwar Khan,
who taught me to reach for excellence.
—R.K.

This book is dedicated to
Michael, Maite and Mercedes.
—L.F. & R.J.

I can't walk and I can't run. But I can fly.

On the morning of Basunt, the skies above Lahore are teeming with kites, like so many souls trying to reach heaven.

Even before dawn lights the east, I rise. Quickly I dress and drag myself across the floor. I head straight for the roof, up two flights of stairs to the chair that awaits me, like a throne ready for its king. All but the faithful still sleep.

I want the day to begin, but for now I must wait. I need help to get my kite into the air, but once it's up, I'm king of the skies. Ha, ha!

My kite is small, yet built for speed. It's the best kite I've ever built. Made of bamboo and tissue paper, it has two long streamers as tails, but they look more like legs. I call it *Guddi Chore*, which means Kite Thief. For that is what it is.

I've waited all year for Basunt. It is the one day I am better than anyone else. The one time I win.

I take out my special string, a hundred metres of the strongest twine. I rubbed it all with powdered glass till it was sharp enough to cut. This is the secret to being a good kite thief.

When my sister arrives I let out enough string for her to carry my kite to the edge of the roof. "Don't step on the tails!" I cry. "Be careful! There should be no holes in it."

She nods. If we are lucky, we will capture some of the kites, and she knows she'll get her share.

On the count of three she leaps as high as she can while I tug on the string. *Guddi Chore* bites into the breeze and starts to climb. My heart soars with it, higher than my kite ever will. Higher and higher, where no legs can go.

6

Time to attack. My sister rubs her hands in anticipation.

The first kite I target belongs to the bully next door. His kite is so huge I nickname it Goliath. It must have cost a fortune.

I work the string, dipping *Guddi Chore* so it will circle the giant.

Being so big, Goliath is slow. The bully tries to veer away, but in no time I have him. My kite string rubs his kite string, like a knife cutting through *ghee*.

Snip. I have sliced it.

Ha, ha! Goliath flies free, and my neighbour's string drops from the sky.

The bully is angry, but he should not be. I fought fair.

He takes out another kite. A better one, perhaps even better than *Guddi Chore*. He gets it climbing, riding the rising currents of air, till it is almost as high as mine.

I take a deep breath and wait.

He circles, trying to trap *Guddi Chore*.

I move away. Ha, ha! He shall not win. My higher rooftop gives me the advantage. I hold *Guddi Chore* still, waiting for the next attack.

He veers his kite to the left, trying to circle.

Quickly I pull as hard as I can, sending *Guddi* into a steep dive.

"Let up!" yells my sister. "You'll crash."

Just before *Guddi* hits I pull up and around, several times, tangling the bully's line so he cannot get it free. Gently I pull his kite in, till my sister can reach it.

My neighbour is even more angry, but there is nothing he can do. His cut string is like a fishing line with nothing on the hook.

I move on to other kites. They are prey, ready to be plucked from the sky.

Big kites, little kites,
fancy and plain. Red kites,
blue kites, even kites made
of old newspaper.

With my brother stationed
many blocks downwind,
some of the kites we have
freed will become ours.

He comes to our rooftop
all through the day, to carry
them up. My sister stacks
them in a pile.

Now I'm attacking them in groups, making wide circles around clusters of them. Like a scythe in a field of wheat I slash through the trembling strings, setting them free. For a while they can fly where the wind takes them.

When they descend, as they must, they belong to whoever finds them. But at least they have tasted freedom.

Sometimes loose kites come close enough for me to catch. Circling them, like a spider with a fly, I tangle their strings and draw them in.

My sister catches some too, snaring their strings with a long bamboo pole topped with thorns.

If I am king, she is queen of the sky.

At the end of the day we have a big pile. I choose the three that I want. Then my brother and sister get their pick.

When they have chosen, they start back down the stairs.

My sister asks if I will come too.

No. Not yet.

The sun is setting on a glorious day. I want to stay up here to watch, to feel the cool breeze. To make my day last a little longer.

Then a strange sound rises from the alley below.

Hauling myself over to the parapet, I look down.

A young girl trudges through the mud, sobbing, trailing a kite string behind her.

I think that was the sound I heard, but I cannot see her face. It is bent low toward the ground.

Something makes me reach over to my pile of kites, choose a pretty green one and drop it over the side of the roof. It floats, slicing the air side to side, to land close beside her.

The crying stops. She runs to the kite and picks it up. I duck just as she looks up to see where it came from.

When I dare to look again, she is skipping along. Then she rounds the corner and is gone.

One by one the stars come out, shining down like a million jewelled kites. I am no longer lord of the skies. My day is done.

Time to join my sister and brother. Together we will tell our parents of the triumphs of *Guddi Chore*.

And tomorrow I will begin planning for next year, next Basunt, when I will reign again.

Basunt

In early February, when the trees of Lahore, Pakistan, burst into bloom and light breezes carry the fresh scent of spring, it's time for Basunt, the annual kite festival. It started many years ago with the Hindu celebration of the end of the cool weather and the beginning of spring. With time it became a celebration that crossed religious and cultural differences.

People from outlying areas flock to the city to see the splendid sights and kite battles. Many kite enthusiasts spend weeks preparing for the festival, practising their flying skills by waging mock fights in the skies over Lahore.

Many string vendors use parks to prepare the kite string — the main weapon in the kite matches. They need room to stretch the string between poles to ready it for battle.

Nowadays, the festivities begin on the eve of Basunt. Using huge searchlights perched on rooftops so they can see, people fly white kites — white shows up best in the night sky. When day comes, they bring out the colourful kites. Shouts and cheers, drumming and bugle blasts mix with gunshots to set the festive mood. Everywhere there is feasting and parties. Women dress in bright colours, often wearing yellow to symbolize spring.

It was while standing on a rooftop in January, peeling oranges and watching one of these practice fights, that I first got the idea for *King of the Skies*.